MW01277184

CONIUM
REVIEW
vol. 7

Conium Press
Portland, OR

The Conium Review
Vol. 7
© 2018 Conium Press
Portland, OR

http://www.coniumreview.com

ISBN-10 1-942387-11-3
ISBN-13 978-1-942387-11-4
ISSN 2164-6252

Cover Image: © GlobalP / iStock
Layout & Design: James R. Gapinski

THE CONIUM REVIEW
vol. 7

James R. Gapinski
Managing Editor

Maryse Meijer
Contest Judge

Holly Lopez
Associate Editor

[contents]

[contents]

A MERMAID
VISITS
REXALL DRUGS

Suzanne Burns

A MERMAID VISITS REXALL DRUGS

Suzanne Burns

Sometimes it's easier this way, to hide my guilt where no one really knows me, wrapped in a white paper sack stapled shut to protect my privacy.

For an hour each week, my legs come back. The first time I grew legs, days after my sailor brought me to shore, me pretending to be rescued because even a sea creature knows every man needs to pretend to rescue every woman, I marveled at their vocation. To walk. To run. To climb into hips and the secret pact women hide between their thighs; to flare into such majestic toes, ten resilient stones designed to meet the hardness of the world. Now I don't really notice: legs, toes, fins, tail, only tools to raise me out of the salty backyard pool to my favorite place on earth.

There are no pharmacies where I come from. There isn't much of anything where I come from, but shells. Down there of course we wear shell bras. And too many shell bracelets and necklaces to count. We even have shell lamps with real shell shades but nowhere to plug them in. Up here, you have drugstores with lipstick no tide will wash away. Soda fountains with so many flavors of ice cream. Wart remover, hair gel, an unending field of cotton balls.

For my sailor, each week I buy a box of Old Spice then stack the cologne like red bricks under the bathroom sink. To stay loyal to him because I am loyal to him, mostly because I hardly ever leave my pool, and he does barbecue close to the deep end, handing me my dinner on a real plate with a real napkin that doesn't stay dry for very long.

But the sole reason for one hour a week I don't miss my dorsal fin is fish oil. Omega-3 fatty acids in my purse, in the highest dose possible, and the pharmacist never asks.

The first dose, two pills shining in my palm like precious jelly, I take in the parking lot before I even start my car. When no one is looking. While my legs begin to numb, and I know its time to head home. The more pills I take, the louder my heart beats, strong, steady, harmonizing with my bones as they arc into the hidden white wonder of configuration. My hair grows long, and I let it grow longer after each 500 milligram swallow, so long, sometimes all the next door neighbor sees from his window are my blonde highlights floating out across the water.

But as I float, displaced from Sirenum scopuli, smelling now of Jovan Island Gardenia Cologne and coconut Lip Smackers, I do wonder if I've just swallowed someone I used to know. That one Skipjack tuna I loved for a summer as we swam together in the pelagic zone, his rough corselet rubbing against my eager blue fins, all the promises I thought I heard him whisper through so many bubbles, all the promises I swore to almost keep.

WHAT CAN I GET YOU?

Chelsea Harris

Chelsea Harris

Taco Bell. Crushed ice. Diet Dr. Pepper. Gas stations galore. Plastic wrappers. The Golden Arches. Yellow lines. Him saying Buckle up, buttercup, click it or ticket, his hand on my knee. Slurpees. Purple tongues. I have to pee. Rest stop vending machines. Him holding the truck door open, his hand on my ass as I climb back in. Smells. Smells from the engine, smells from our bodies, smells from the grease punching through paper bags in the backseat. His hand moving from my knee to my thigh to my crotch. Pulling off at Exit 23. His fingers strumming the steering wheel. Him saying, Didn't think I knew how to play the guitar, eh? Sweat pooling. Radio humming. Something classic. AC blasting. My shins freezing. Pulling up to the drive-thru. What can I get you? Two cheeseburgers and a side of fries and a large Coke and freedom, please. Bulging bellies. Walmart. The beauty aisle. Tubes of mascara. Everything coated in hard plastic. Him rounding the corner. The look in his eyes. Him saying That shade would do you nicely, baby. Him saying Let me get that for you. Me knowing he has to because I've got no money. That game we play. Cigarettes at the check-out. Cans spilling from the bed of the truck.

His daddy's ashes in the backseat. Mile marker 157. Mile marker 162. Miles and miles to go. Rivers to cross. The French King Bridge. Him pulling over, daring me to jump. Him not knowing if he wanted me dead or alive. Us in the motel bathroom, bodies slick with steam. His chest hair rubbing my back raw. A gunshot in the distance. Rabbits, he says, they hunting rabbits. Infomercials. Game shows. That empty glow of the TV at three AM. Him snoring next to me. Me thinking what if I went outside to smoke. Me thinking what if I walked to the truck. Me thinking what if I walked to the road. Me thinking what if I hitched a ride out of here. His dick flopped over on his leg. His mouth wide open.

In the morning, we drove the rest of the way. He stopped at a diner on the way out, ordered a chicken fried steak with a side of breakfast potatoes and two sunny side-up eggs. I ate his toast. He said once we got there he was going to ask me to marry him. He said all he wanted was to make his daddy proud. I thought, what a fucking joke. If I had any money at all I'd be in New York, in Chicago, somewhere out there, somewhere with meaning. But I knew I'd say I do. I knew we'd end up driving the whole way back. I knew we'd take over his daddy's business. Live in his daddy's house. Knew I'd make him pot roast and fuck him in his parent's bed until we had kids, until we got old, until I drove myself right back to that bridge and finally made that decision for him.

THE ENDANGERED

FISH

OF THE

COLORADO

RIVER

INNOVATIVE SHORT FICTION CONTEST WINNER

Emily Wortman-Wunder

INNOVATIVE SHORT FICTION CONTEST WINNER

Emily Wortman-Wunder

Colorado pikeminnow. *Ptychochelius lucius.* Slender, cylindrical, with an endless body and a long, pointed snout. Once so abundant it was the poor man's meat, it was devastated by dams and invasive species. Predicted to go extinct in my son's lifetime but, as it happened, outlived him.

Once the fish grew big as deer and filled the rivers so thickly you could hear them swimming from shore. So say the old timers, at least, the ones who gave it its first name: the squawfish. Even into college, Max would call it that, to needle me—"You and your mamby pamby PC pikeminnow," he would say slyly—but also, I think, he just loved that name the best. The way it squawks off the tongue, two brash syllables to the prim mouthful of what we call it now. I secretly agreed, despite its history, despite the misogyny and racism twisted into it like runoff in a river. The squawfish always felt like *my* fish: the subject of my senior project, my master's thesis, my early years of fieldwork; I was working on the squawfish when I met the engineer. In the long dry years after Max was born the fish was renamed the Colorado pikeminnow, but that name always felt like it belonged to someone else.

Perhaps what Max always accused me of was right: I wanted to turn back the clock.

Max as a baby was gummy, devoted, irresistible. The way his starfish fingers reached out to grab my eyes, the way he grunted as he nursed, the way he crawled into bed with us in the middle of the night, all the way into kindergarten. The way he adored Russian fairy tales and colored pencils and baby birds. The way he would line up all of our shoes, pair after pair, curving over the sill and out the door. All of this, and I still felt the pull of the river like an undercurrent of despair. I thought I would never be able to leave him, until I did.

I was an inappropriate mother from the start. Squawfish, I explained when Max was way too young, means, roughly, cuntfish. Trash fish. Fish as easy to reap as the tribal women; like them, though, it held something of itself in reserve. Given half a sandbar and a bit of flood, the pikeminnow made its comeback as stealthy as a woman slipping back into her old haunts. Like me.

This was the story of my life, the one for which I thought Max would eventually forgive me: left my dream job to marry an engineer, had his baby, lived a sensible decade buried in the suburbs and then, against all odds, clawed my way back to work with the pikeminnow, its resurgence mirroring my own.

Bonytail chub. *Gila elegans*. A large cyprinid fish of the Colorado river, growing up to two feet long and reproducing rarely, if at all. Like most desert fish, it is dark above and pale beneath, hidden in both directions. Tail so thin and bony that even nine-year-old Max could grab one in his hand and hoist it from the water.

"How come we never find any little ones?" he asked, and long before I finished telling him about dams and age classes and functionally extinct he had wandered off, bored of me already. "I'm still talking," I yelled after him. He shrugged as he disappeared into the sage.

His boredom was a weapon, a silent protest against how I made him come to Utah every summer as part of the custodial agreement. "The river is the world as it ought to be," I'd tell him. He would sit shotgun in my pickup and not say a word for 362 miles as we drove up out of the city, across the mountains, and down into the desert. As soon as we hit camp he would slip away, liquid and alive; he'd chase lizards, pocket arrowheads, and throw rocks endlessly across the water, enjoying it the way I hoped he would. But the instant he caught me watching he'd go sullen.

I spent my off-hours straightening his Scooby Doo sleeping bag, rigging the Dutch oven so that we could make pizza on the fire, loading him up with ring pops and firecrackers and s'mores. Still, one mistake and he'd be bitterly against me. "You care about your stupid fish more than me," he'd say, kicking at the fire. "That's why I love Dad more than I love you."

"Did you put him up to this?" I once demanded of my ex, near tears. Through the phone I heard him push his woodworking goggles to the top of his head and sigh before he answered. I could picture the soft sweaty dents beneath his eyes, the sharp smell of cut wood, the way he'd brush the sawdust from his beard before answering, and I had a wave of longing so acute it almost knocked me down.

I could hear him carefully distancing himself from his bitterness. My fault, I knew, but I refused to allow myself regret. The fish had no use for patio projects, soccer games, vegetable gardens, or the-game-on-Sunday life, and I had chosen the fish, or what was left of them.

"Max is just a kid," he said at last. "This is about him being nine."

Nine, ten, eleven, twelve: every year I hoped that this would be the one Max learned to love the river, love camping, love me. Instead he perfected the art of the preteen pout. He dropped my gear into the water, my clothes into the fire, my food into the sand. He ran away when I got out the sunscreen and then howled in pain and rage when his back was too raw to sleep. I told myself this was natural; I told myself he would grow out of it. I told myself the nights of sobbing would be worth it in the end.

What Max loved instead was his Gameboy and the bunk bed his dad had built him back in Denver; his TV shows, Domino's pizza and sushi. He loved telling me about all of the things he did with his dad, and all of the things that I did not do, or was doing wrong, or would never understand. "You just don't get me, Mom," he said, in a world-weary imitation of something he'd heard on TV.

"Nor you me," I snapped back.

The bonytail chub, like all cyprinid fish, has a sensory organ other fish don't have. In the end, it was like I sensed the river with an organ that Max and my ex did not possess. I loved the sweat, the stink, the river's algal pull; the slime of the fish, the alkali of the salt flats on either side, the ancient sandstone stained with iron; the ruins, the petroglyphs, the hidden canyons hung with vines. It mystified me that they didn't love it, too.

Now I sit alone in my camp chair after dusk, my daily notes fallen to one side, the tang of DEET keeping the mosquitoes at bay. The air shifts and a breeze pulls along the canyon, bringing the scent of nylon tent and my dinner, a can of maple baked beans cranked open and eaten cold. I once assumed the river was vast enough to be my everything. Now that it is all I have, I find that it is not.

Humpback chub. *Gila cypha*. Evolved to swim the fast waters of the desert river and specialized to breed only in water warm to the touch. Possesses a distinctive swollen hump just above the head. Almost entirely scaleless; back is greenish gray, sides silver, belly white.

The Humpback Chub has thrived in the recent drought, even as other species have suffered and declined. My colleagues cheer and roar into my winter office with grins as wide as the beers they buy to celebrate. I go along, I chink beer neck to beer neck; I even, when called upon, make speeches about persistence and science and learning to let natural systems do their work.

I believe all that, but the last conversation I ever had with Max lingers in my ears. "A couple of fish, Mom?" he said to me, tapping salsa from his chip, his carpentry-calloused pinky curved delicately toward me, as if defining the space he was going to need. "Four fish? That's why you walked out on Dad and me?"

"I never walked out on *you*," I said, my own burrito ashes in my mouth. That was two months before his car failed to negotiate a curve and rammed into a tree, and I never had a chance to explain it further.

I worked for you, I would have said, *so you can have a richer world*, and he would have rolled his eyes. "Things change," he might have said. "You can't stop time, you know."

For so long, I lived upon my certainty. But now I doubt. When I think of the recovery of the Humpback Chub, all I can remember is how by the end Max and I had almost made it. There were lunches, texts, and phone calls; he talked of making a trip to try the rock climbing spots near my old field camp. But as if on cue, I put the fish between us every time. "Aren't you even a little bit glad you got the chance to grow up in God's own paradise?" I once asked him, teasingly.

He considered it carefully, the way he did everything, rubbing the bridge of his nose with the knuckle of his thumb. "Utah made me what I am today," he said at last, "So I give it that. But what I remember was not a paradise."

Razorback sucker. *Xyrauchen texanus.* Distinctive flat bottom and humped back; will grow to a meter long and look like it swallowed a boat. Oliveaceous brown above and pale yellow beneath. Smooth.

The Razorback was Max's favorite fish. Even on the sulkiest days of his teen hegemony, he would pop up in a moment if we had a razorback in the nets and come over from where he was grumping on the shore about not having service for his phone or not having pizza in camp for dinner. He'd crouch, walking on the slick stones in his sandals as if born to it, his gray eyes intent on the prize, his growing shoulder blades blistering beneath the desert sun.

Once in college he came along on a survey day. "I still think you eco-freaks are just afraid of change," he said, stooping over the net while his breath blew out in frosty clouds, "But if I had to save one thing from 1872, I think I would reach in and rescue this."

The sudden resurgence of the Razorback in 2014 shocked everyone and made wildlife headlines all around the world; no matter how far the news traveled, though, it would never find its way to Max. I whispered it to the air instead. "They found some little ones, Max," I said. "In nine of 47 sites. The highest return in years."

I even made a pilgrimage back to the city, visited the gravestone with its strange clean edges. I stood under the puny hybrid maple tree and leaned in close, but when I opened my mouth, other words came out, raging and lost against the wind. "This is change, Max," I whispered. "*This* is change."

The wind whipped my words away.

LOVE.
SHOO.
GO AWAY.

Sonal Sher

Sonal Sher

And then I was in love. It was a surprise. I had not expected the animal to come to me. I thought I was done with it. I had domesticated it already. Love was for those who were searching. The ones who wanted to be saved. What was it doing with me?

It had begun as all stories do. Boy meets girl. Girl meets boy. Only that I don't remember where we had met. Or what either of us had said. In that precise moment, none of this mattered. Of all the wonderful anecdotes that I could have told to construct a spectacular me, instead I just sat and sipped on my tea. Or was it coffee? They both tasted like a faint reflection of themselves in that day, so how does it matter? There were a few faces around. They too sipped on their beverages. Tea. Coffee. Black coffee. Black coffee without sugar. Strong tea without sugar. Seasonal juice. Watermelon in autumn.

I had arrived with a cloud over my head. It was only covering my face for now. My body was still free to move. There were no monsoons, just unexpected intermittent rainfall that would drench me once a while. Didn't help that the weather department never functioned accurately inside my brain. It would announce sunshine, but a cyclone would appear out of the blue. It didn't have a sense of humor about its inefficiencies either.

It's not my fault. It's global warming, it would say.

Outside, the nature seemed to agree. It wailed too, for a day or two at least. I was drenched inside out. And so there was nothing to do but sit down quietly and drink my tea/coffee. The boy, he drank both coffee and tea at first. Some of the faces found it cute. Other made a joke about it. There was a two-minute conversation woven around this very quirk every time we ordered beverages in the future. I did not find it particularly funny.

Unnecessary, I thought. Why can't he just make up his mind?

For only a micro-second I was perplexed by this question, but before my irritation could rise of indignation the clouds darkened. I was consumed by the weather again. I sighed and continued to sip on my nameless beverage. It was time, and one by one the faces got up. Some did it slowly. Certain others were eager to rush. My brain did not record which one he was, but in a few seconds I found myself standing next to him. Something struck me immediately.

You are tall.

The words flew out of my mouth before I could leash them in. He nodded in agreement. We walked together to the destination. He asked, I answered. Formal enquires were made. Job. City. Work. I remember none of it now. It is a memory. I accept for it is sharp, the brain of mine. It always remembers things as they happen. But it never knows what is happening.

The cloud stayed for only a week. I don't quite remember when it moved away. Maybe it was the sixth day. All I know is that I was still drinking tea then. The story was in the time period that can be safely termed as A.C.

After Coffee.

Was it the coffee that invoked the first beast? I don't know. I had switched without reason. When in Rome, kind of an analogy. A break from the lemongrass scented tea and the hot espresso that was life otherwise. I returned to an old love—filter coffee—poured between two utensils. Back and forth, back and forth until it was just right to touch my lips. Maybe I did invoke the beast when I switched.

The first animal knocked on my door soon after. A familiar beast. Nothing to be afraid of. It didn't visit often, but I always did recognize the sounds of its steps. And I adored it despite its vicious frivolity. Despite its magnanimous appetite. In spite of its prima donna ways. But the one thing I didn't quite like about it is that was that it never slept. It hibernated for days, months, even years, but once it was awake it was always alert. And always hungry.

It demanded all of my attention. All the time.

It didn't matter to begin with. There was so much to feed it. My mind was ripe with food. Conscious and sub-conscious, the beast was free to eat what it wanted. It never quite felt satiated for more than a few minutes, and yet it was just pure joy to watch it devour everything in sight. And then it happened. It was on the day I learned the meaning of the word estuary. The boy had said something innocuous at my appearance.

Your outfit looks like the Greek sea.

I was wearing blue. And pink. Shades of both in a drizzle of white. For a second, the words took me to a foreign land that was filled with shades of blue and pink, sprinkled with white sand. In my mind, Greece transformed into the most dazzling spot in the universe. And for a brief moment, I stood next to the sea, my feet firm on the sand and calling out to the waves. The waves swept my senses. Obstructed my chain of reason. The animal had caught a fancy for him.

His neck to be precise. It wanted to chew it to bones.

I knew that this moment would pass. It was a moment in the series of moments that would eventually become an anecdote of desire. Of untasted skin and unexplained motivations. But for that moment, it had become everything and there was nothing to be done. I wasn't worried still. It's good to have a direction. Animals want something to play with. Someone to play with. For today, it is him.

I fed it all I could. I wove tales for it. The tales were short. Flash fiction. A splash of neck. The rhythmic movement of legs. The buzzing of voice. The unending long limbs.

I fed it everything I could forage. We were the gatherers after all, I thought to myself. Least I could do was gather and feed.

So I made a tent around the neck. At the precise point where the edge of an ear, the delicate slope of the earlobe, met the nape. It was here that we stayed. The beast and I. Every morning we would roam the surroundings, sniffing for food. We wandered away from the exaggerated real world and to the taste of warm salty skin. One day I set up a tub there and immersed the beast into the warm water. For hours. Till the pores were plump with moisture. I thought that when it would finally emerge, the hollow of hunger would not be empty anymore.

But it wasn't satisfied.

So I ran a train across his limbs. It travelled slowly, engine spewing cloud—not dark, they were rose colored blue. The beast sat next to me, his head outside the window the air passing through his face.

And yet it wanted more.

I made a clay toy of him with my eyes. His fingers were coarse, just enough to scratch every cell on my skin.

I reconstructed his Adam's apple.

I painted his chest in the color red.

But the beast became hungrier with every passing minute. It ate and ate. It ate every single glance. It ate the whiff of the perfume. It gobbled the edge of the collarbone. It howled as it never had, and I could barely keep up. For the faces too demanded my attention, a part of my brain that was not consumed by this animal. The crumbs of my body that stored away the pain had to be dusted out.

I spoke with the faces, making conversation about homelessness and belonging. Of loneliness and green forests with ironic names. I even spoke of love, searching for it under the mud. In my diary. In the past. But I never found it there. I had never written it down. I had stored it in a metal pencil box with a cartoon on the cover and it was back home, in the drawer by the window.

The conversation about love turned to sunlight and tea. To homecoming. To eternity. To trust.

And then the innocuous became dangerous. Blue became shades of blue. Jokes became inside jokes. Tea turned to coffee.

In only a few seconds in the world. A few hours in another. A few years in the place that the beast resided. He was the same animal, he and I. Mine was angry.

His? I didn't ask. What if it was angry too?

I deflected my path and took another street. I stayed

silent. Meditating over watermelon juice and whiskey. From that day on, I drank whiskey.

It had been only three full days since the beast had arrived. But slowly I was turning from master to slave. From an intelligible host to a blabbering fool. I only slept for a few hours every day. And as soon as I would open my eyes, I would immediately begin to forage. To feed.

This too will pass I told myself with confidence. Only a few more days and it will end. Sure it was tiring, but it was still fun. Like the endless celebration between Christmas and New Year. But it didn't pass. I was exhausted. My eyes, they pained. Chillies. My brain, it counted the number of drinks. The puffs of green smoke. What it didn't count was the hollow inside me that was rising up. And had finally settled under my eyelids. Slowly burning out. Evaporating slowly.

I would often imagine that saying the words out loud would make it better.

You are a beautiful man.

Just to say these words would be enough because then the burden wouldn't be mine anymore. But to say those words would be the end of everything. I was scared.

I sought help. Therapy. Talking it out might help.

'Why don't you do something about it?' asked my friend innocently.

'Why don't I do something about it?' I repeated the question to myself unsure of the answer.

Is it because I am monogamous? That would have been the simplest answer to give. And yet it didn't feel right. For my brain was not being monogamous. My body was crying for a solution that my answer could not provide.

I was of course afraid to follow my instincts. A part of me didn't want to shatter my exhausting world. It was too perfect, my fantasy. What we had built, my animal and I, it was poetry. It was art. Was the real kiss going to feel like a thousand thunder storms? Would the hands feel rough against my soft skin? Would the breath smell of faint musk?

I was a coward. I was too afraid to find out.

So we spent the night talking of our bodies, my friend and I. We spoke of lovers—had and had again. Of unsure hands and slobbery kisses. Of the difference between stench and smell. Of aggression and possession. Of sex and fucking. It was a night of longing and disappointment. In the morning I woke up refreshed.

I think I am recovering, I said to my friend. It is getting tired, the beast; it will fall asleep soon.

How?

I don't know.

I was bluffing of course. Trying to make myself believe in something that I really wanted to believe. Repeat it enough times and your brain will accept. It's gone. It's gone. It will soon be gone. But the fucking bastard didn't go away. Instead, it invited a friend along. Someone I had not met in over a decade.

It is strange the things this new animal fed on. A bowl of noodles. Sunlight. Anger. It found all of them here. Invoked by serendipity, it appeared from thin air. A ghost of the past that I had safely left behind. I could not believe my eyes. Was it real? No. It couldn't be so. As it always happens, it arrived a little late. Only at the precise minute when he was moving away. Without a goodbye. Such a cliché, my brain told me. I agreed.

Such a cliché.

I looked at the second beast.

What am I going to do with you?

The beast was blind. It did not notice that I was looking at it. Staring it down with a quiet confusion. What kind of stupid animal arrives to a party uninvited? That too in the last five minutes. But it wasn't even listening. It was too busy following his scent down to the street till it got faint and finally mixed up with the smell of sunlight.

He disappeared. No last touch. A warm hug. A glance? Like life and death it began and ended, unwanted and inconvenient. I knew that it would happen one day—I had waited for it but it stung like a motherfucker.

What am I going to do with you? I asked again to the second beast.

It didn't care to respond and lounged comfortably, making a home around me. Or was it meditating? I don't know. But its very presence made me angry. I wanted it gone. I filled my pipe and smoked. Maybe the smoke would bother it and it would dissolve. Maybe it was an aberration. Maybe I was intoxicated. The drinking could be having its effect at last. But it didn't go away. The hollow became a crater and filled up with autumn leaves. Winter.

They say that the nights are the worst, but it didn't feel so. It was the days that had me gripped by the throat. They spread through my lungs like smoke but not with the faint intoxication of relief. I could barely breathe. I shook my head to shake up my mind. Breathe in. Breathe out. Breathe in. Breathe out. The body was functioning as expected.

Everything is fine, reported the brain.

And yet.

At first I called it an infection. One of those flus that reign over you for three days like a fucking poison. But every infection has to run its course. And so I waited.

Patiently.

Then I called it a condition. Like the dark cloud. Both did affect some place in the center of my chest, only that the symptoms were exact opposite.

Maybe a run will push it out my brain suggested.

And so I ran. I ran to the end of the river. I ran to the top of the mountain. I ran back home.

A few days have gone by. Now I am troubled. This animal is a stray, it shouldn't be here, one crumb of my brain argues with the other. What if the owners cause trouble? Is it a pet friendly building? And even if it is, the point is that I don't want it.

Shoo. Go away.

The animal doesn't budge. I see it waiting in the corridor, observing me, silently. Still meditating. Omnipresent. Like watermelon. I walk out and close the door behind me. It follows me. It doesn't bark. But its nails scratch the tiles of the floor making a delicious sound. It rings in the pit of my stomach and rises up to my lungs. I struggle. I take a deep breath. Breathe in. Breathe out.

What am I supposed to do with you? I ask frustrated.

It walks into my lap uninvited and sinks down. It is not going anywhere I realize. Maybe it doesn't need to. So what if he is gone.

LEGS

Matt Kolbet

LEGS

Matt Kolbet

When legs first disappeared, no one saw an accident, the literal world colliding, but an opening of fate's cosmic jar. Castigation. A moral test failed, perhaps.

A man appeared in a hospital missing both legs and an explanation.

There were no signs of assault, no saw or bite marks, only smooth edges like polished alabaster where his legs had been. Medical records showed he'd been born fully formed, symmetrical. The doctors didn't want to freeze frame it by writing anything up, for people are always feeling as if their legs have been cut from under them, during romantic breakups or election cycles or reading, for their first time, a hospital bill.

The man who lost his lower limbs woke to tell his wife he could no longer go to work. She thought he was joking, complaining because the holidays were over and it hadn't snowed, when she saw, or rather did not see, his mislaid legs. She drove him to the hospital where they charged several hundred dollars to sit in a room. Staring at white walls, he contemplated how fortunate this was. Otherwise he would have sat at home, worried and without answers, for free.

His doctors hemmed and hawed, uncertain if the transformation would be fatal. After all, following a lifetime of sight, some people went blind, the world suddenly darkness or impenetrable white, needing a hand to limp through the rest of their days. As the man's stare deepened, they attempted jokes—he didn't have a leg to stand on—and tempered it with a notion: it wasn't legs but what was between them that mattered. It could have been worse. Without his wife, he'd be left to lower himself to the ground, the first step toward burial.

They didn't wish to extend his stay (room rates weren't hourly) though they'd never seen such a case, not in medical journals or escapist reading, worlds where people weren't just blood and bone, where characters worried over a distant expression in their lover's eyes, a look the doctors understood well. Today wasn't their first medical mystery. Nevertheless, it wasn't every day a man came to them, his legs having inexplicably run off on their own.

The next morning there were a dozen identical instances of lost limbs, sparing the doctors credible explanations. A hundred cases followed by lunch. A hundred more. Absences grew.

When pressed, the head of the hospital lifted his chin and in a haughty tone suggested it must be an extended trial. Everyone ought to straighten up as best they could.

Teachers and plumbers and accountants and car salesmen and judges all suffered AWOL legs. Not everyone suffered equally, though. Robes hid a magistrate's body, and it was usual for defendants to feel justice was nothing but hot air, borne of an empty judge, soulless beneath the robes. It was difficult, however, to sell cars when you couldn't operate the pedals. Strapped in like an infant, you risked kidnap by a full-limbed customer with a diabolical sense of whimsy. After working hours, life got worse. By Friday, mounting losses divided cities into two camps. The power of legs was motility and reach (expensive wines and gadgets lurked on the highest shelves). Others begged for dregs from bottles, table scraps, and toddler's toys. To paraphrase a more universally-known adage, in a legless world the one-legged man is king.

Except it wasn't true. As legs vanished through the middle of the week, numbers tilted. Crawling hordes looked to knock walkers over. Anger and jealousy require nothing but a heart. Those with legs hid. If they had to go out, it was in wheelchairs, their lower halves hidden by blankets. The head of the hospital declared the examination over. Forgetting his previous words, he said divine probity had, in record time, made its choice clear.

While he was proven right, subsequent changes had nothing to do with his pronouncement. People gathered in the streets. Patient zero, a title he embraced as he counted legs, watched families caught in mutual tragedy quit fighting over curfews or chores. Others struck the earth, hoping to spawn an earthquake so the planet might swallow or cast them up again. All their lives, pounding desks for emphasis, hitting windows out of anger, it had been the same impetus. People crawled to confession, at last seeing eye to eye. Nothing could be done without supplication, atonement for assaulting others with delayed fates, the gods' will eternally shrouded in mystery.

Those with nothing to confess (or whose sins were inextricable, unlike their legs) met together to re-map rooms, buildings, cities. The intellectual ritual became a pragmatic campaign to re-assess the world's texture, a spectrum from whipped strawberries to marble. Despite these labors, no maps were ever completed. Whether the world was afraid to disclose its hidden islands, or the experiment had changed, the universe shifted again.

One morning, eight days after the initial disappearance, the legless began gliding. More than bodies swimming on skateboards or creepers searching out problems under a car, people floated toward one another, no higher than waist level. They kissed their hellos and shook with hands no longer needed to pull weighty torsos over gravelly earth. It seemed simple. They might have been doing it forever.

Still, it is no surprise when legs re-appeared just over a week later, affixed as though they'd never gone, people changed once more. No one could imagine anything as ridiculous as vanished limbs, so essential to movement (even blind men stumble about with feet attached, ready to obey). No one remembered how to spell rectitude. No one was surprised at how people ran, whooping in celebration, turning to strike one another, not needing canons for saints or munitions. Their legs were sufficient. Neighborhoods became hurricanes of brawling feet and rocks, passersby punting stones towards elevated heads. Even the first victim, his gaze distant, kicked his wife under the sheets, and joined those damn fools who act like they control more than their own towering globe.

CASTAWAYS

Bridget Apfeld

CASTAWAYS

Bridget Apfeld

On the night we dug up the girl in the bottle, my sister's boyfriend Cat smashed a brick through the windshield of her Pontiac. It happened while we were at dinner, all four of us around the kitchen table: my mother and my stepfather, my sister Sarah, and I. Nobody seemed to be eating much—just passing around dishes and picking like thieves at the edges—but that was how it always was in our family: we preferred to do things from the corners of our eyes. We were quiet people, all of us.

It happened very quickly: my stepfather Gene at the sink, filling up his glass; my mother with her hand on the back of his empty chair; Sarah and I sat with our backs to the window, so we looked into the dim house. There was the gravely noise of a car slowing down outside, though I may have imagined that later. My stepfather drank his glass at the sink, rinsed it, filled it again.

Then there was a terrible crashing sound. The shredding noise of a car making smoke down the street.

"Jesus God," my stepfather said, at the window.

"Don't tell me," my mother said. She held a hand to her eyes and said, again, "Don't tell me. Please, just don't."

"What is it?" I begged. I twisted in my seat. I had none of my mother's reticence about possible horrors of the world; I waited up every night to watch the news with my parents, hungry for the grainy images depicting sorrow and tragedy both local and national. I wanted to be shocked, frightened, and then comforted.

"Sicko," Sarah said to me. She sat still, though there was a pulse in her throat. "Just be quiet." At seventeen, five years my elder, my sister did not like to show when she was afraid, but it could make her mean.

Outside it was nearly dark. It was late October, and a pale light fled down through the trees. The trunks were black bars and the sky was smooth and clear. It was the time of day when automatic garage lights were just now turning on, and down the street I could see small patches of our neighbors' homes, though there were not many. We lived some distance from town on a winding road in the wood, and most people around us were there because they did not want to know anyone that closely, wanted to live some sort of separate life from everything around them.

The hole in Sarah's car window was almost perfectly square, like a cartoon hole. The ground around the door didn't glitter with shards of glass like I thought it might, but I could hear her boots crunch against something sharp. I sidled up next to her and very carefully leaned forward, letting myself fall against the car with flat palms, so I could look into the window. A gray brick, like a slab from a walkway, sat on the seat.

"Bunch of punks, probably," I said. I'd heard recently in school about bands of marauding punks, meth heads and coked out dropouts who drove up and down the roads looking for trouble, and I was pleased to find evidence in our driveway.

"Sure," she said. I didn't think she sounded particularly convinced, so I said again, "Punks, Sarah. They're all over the place."

Gene came up, shone his flashlight around. He turned to Sarah. His face was impassive, as it almost always was—a tall and gentle man, my stepfather, not a man who let any emotion or thought ripple up to the surface of his skin—and he seemed to consider something in a measured way before he spoke.

"He do it?" he asked her. She shrugged.

"Might be," she said.

"Should figure that out," he said.

My mother, at the edge of the driveway, called for us to come back.

"Punks," I said, though no one was listening.

Back in the house Sarah and I sat in the family room in front of the television, sharing the lumpier end of the old pleather sofa where it was more comfortable and smelled pleasantly of soup. Sarah had the clicker and was passing through channels aimlessly. She sat with the remote resting loosely on her knee, and she would pause for only a second on each flicker of light before thumbing the remote and switching the screen again—I was not even sure she was watching the screen.

"Turn on the news," I said to Sarah. She ignored me.

I thought of ways I could make her hand it over, but I was distracted myself by the excitement of the smashed car window. I craned over the back of the couch so I could lift the curtains, but it was dark outside, and the only thing I could see was my face, fish-bowled in the glass, so I settled back into the cushion, watching Sarah watch the TV. Though to me she was only my sister, a face I knew like my own, I was aware in a brotherly way that she was beautiful. She had a fever-flush about her; you looked at her and thought her skin might be hot if you touched it, hot and dry. My sister would never be able to hide herself. I was proud of how beautiful my sister was, aware that I was the brother of a coveted girl. I myself looked, strangely, mostly like Gene: big-eared and lanky, snub-nosed. An odd combination that might, my mother told me, smooth out as I grew older. I didn't care much one way or the other.

From the kitchen I could hear my mother and Gene talking but could not make out what they said.

"Think they'll call the police?" I asked Sarah.

"Why would they?" she said. She kept at the clicker, switching the channels. *Wheel of Fortune* whizzed across the screen. A *National Geographic* lion devoured a gazelle.

"The meth heads," I said. "Your car. Ring a bell?"

"There weren't any meth heads," she said.

"Sarah," I said gently. I would be magnanimous about it. "It's all over the news. They got you."

She turned to me then. Her face ghostly in the blue light from the television screen. On it, two tanned women embraced while a studio audience cheered.

"It was Cat," she said. "Cat threw the brick."

I wondered that she would blame him for the smashed window: Cat, nineteen and bold. Long-haired, long-limbed Cat. In the year my sister had dated him, I had determined Cat was the most interesting person I knew, from his Kurt Cobain hair to his job at the quarry crushing stone, from his predilection toward eating enormous sandwiches with shaved raw ham or his declarations, mouth full of said ham, that his politics were "red, man, red like *Commie* red." My sister seemed to look on Cat equally with bemused fondness and detachment, but to me he was fairly near perfection, in the way a tornado is a perfect specimen of weather.

I did not, though, think he could have thrown a brick though her car window, and I told my sister as much. "He's too peaceful," I pointed out. "He's a *pacifist*, dummy."

In the kitchen, suddenly: a sick scummy bubble of silence that popped with Gene's voice, low, methodical. I could not hear it, but I thought my mother was crying.

My sister pressed the clicker. We watched a few seconds of *Seinfeld*; a black screen, a white burst in a split-second of space, then a hundred penguins pressed together in a great revolving circle.

"They keep each other warm like that," Sarah said to me. "The males carry the eggs and balance them on their feet." She had her legs curled up to her chin and her arms hooked around her shins. She looked a little like an egg herself, I thought. Her hair fell over her back like a veil. I suddenly wanted to stroke her hair, like I'd seen my mother sometimes do when Sarah came home very late on the weekends and they both stood in the kitchen together, in front of the fridge, Sarah pressed into the front of my mother's tatty robe. Sarah held, and still. But I did not move to touch her.

Gene's voice, a little louder. My mother opening and shutting cabinets as though she would find something to say in them if she only shut the doors more firmly. The light had fallen completely outside and on the television a pair of boxers grappled, their bodies glistening as they held each other tightly, pummeling one another's heads with thinning enthusiasm.

"Let's go to the quarry," I said. "Let's go find the girl

in the bottle."

"That's not real," Sarah said, her chin on her knees.

"Do you want to stay here?" I asked. The boxers kept on at their fight.

She considered, then unfolded herself.

"There are shovels in the garage," she said. "Don't let Gene see you when you grab them."

.   .   .

Cat had told us about the girl in the glass bottle the month before, one Sunday afternoon, when my mother and Gene were on some errand and Sarah and I lay on our stomachs in the family room, she flipping through the newspaper while I worked a puzzle. Her phone sat on the carpet at an easy distance from her hand, and every so often it lit up and gave a little buzz. I was not allowed to have a phone yet, so I took very sharp notice of what Sarah did with hers. Though she rarely talked on it, and then only to Cat, she was constantly sending messages, little missives—about what, I had no idea. I had considered trying to steal the phone to read her messages, but I knew she would not forgive me that.

A knock at the door; Sarah raised her eyebrows at me.

"Pizza?" I suggested hopefully.

"This is your problem, Sam," she said, getting up from the carpet and heading down the hallway, "you always want the strangest solution." I picked at the puzzle pieces. Her orneriness only sometimes bothered me.

She returned with Cat behind her, leading him by the hand. She was not affectionate with Cat in front of our parents, and I knew, though it had never been said, that it was because they did not like him. Or at least my mother did not: whenever my mother said hello to Cat, I got the feeling she was telling him she wished he were dead.

They stopped in the doorway, Cat leaning on the frame and my sister leaning on him.

"What's up, man?" he said to me. "What's that you're working on?"

"He likes puzzles," Sarah said. She hooked her arm around Cat's waist. He looked down at me good-naturedly.

"Fucking cool," he said.

"Oh," I said, affecting the sort of shrug I'd seen Cat do. "They're ok."

Cat smiled. "Right on," he said. Sarah played with the belt loop on Cat's jeans, tugging the fabric down so a little wedge of his skin, right on his hip, showed; I watched her fingers trace over that paleness.

"I was missing you," she said to him, her hand still moving left, right, over his hip. She scratched a little like she might a dog. He shifted, and I saw a dark ruff of hair scattered on his belly leading up from his waistband. "Missing you," she said again, not bothering to swing back her long fall of hair that had tangled in his denim coat.

Her fingers scratched a bit farther over, a bit farther down. Cat made a sound in the back of his throat; I studied my puzzle. Cat laughed, and I looked up.

"No date tonight, Sam?" he asked. "Where are all the girls for you?"

"None for him yet," Sarah said. "Too young."

"I've got my own business," I said with as much dignity as I could muster. Sarah smiled, and I glared at her.

"I'm sure you do," Cat said. But said with such

seriousness that I didn't doubt his sincerity. And I appreciated that.

Sarah disappeared into the kitchen; Cat sat down next to me on the floor. He crossed his long legs and leaned back on his elbows, gave me a long even look.

"Tell me, Sam," he said. "You'd be honest with me, right?"

"Sure," I said.

"You think Sarah loves me?" he asked.

I was flattered. I didn't even begin to think of an answer, so taken was I by the asking, and by the time I got around to considering the question he shook his head and said, "Oh, never mind, really. Don't worry about it." I began to feel that I had let him down, but his face was pleasant enough, so I shook away the discomfort.

Sarah's phone buzzed where she'd left it on the floor. Cat and I turned to the blinking red light.

"That thing," I said, "is a nuisance." I'd noticed Cat rarely used his phone and felt an offer of solidarity was in order. He looked at the phone for a moment longer.

"Lot of calls?" he said.

"All the dang time," I said, immediately hoping he would not notice the fumbled curse. But he only seemed a little bored, staring blankly at the phone, and I busied myself with the puzzle pieces.

Sarah returned with a can of Coke tucked under her arm and two glasses filled with lazily fizzing dark soda. She handed a glass to Cat, tossed the Coke can at me.

"Mixed the way you like it," she grinned, kneeling on the floor next to Cat. He took a moment to respond, drawn up out of himself by her voice like a lure through deep water, and then he shone to see her face.

"Cheers, baby," he said, and they clinked their glasses

together. I was struck by that gesture; Sarah was my sister, but she was something else too. She was a woman who mixed drinks, a strange creature who stirred the bubbles in her soda with one long red-nailed finger.

"Got a story for you both," Cat said. "Couple guys at work found a girl buried in a glass bottle the other day."

Cat slung rocks in the quarry down off 51, crushing stones with a sledgehammer that he kept in bed of his pickup and that looked, I thought, like it was topped with a skull: so mangled and dented was the head, dark divots like sockets for eyes. He often brought back small stones for me because he knew I liked to keep them in an old shoebox under my bed. And Cat also brought us stories back from the quarry, stories that fairly bristled with omens and machines and the sweat of men who worked with their hands, and that were punctuated with words that made me perk my ears and blush at the same time. I felt that Cat was talking to me from the past and the future both, those times when he'd sit with Sarah and I in the front yard, slapping dust from the knees of his jeans: Sarah listening with that bemused expression on her face, mocking and alert at the same time, and I—what could I say to anyone of the stories Cat told? I lived and died in that quarry with him.

And now, this. We drank our drinks and listened.

"Northbird found her. Dug her up right at the end of the day. He was sifting through some blowoff and saw this big old green thing and pulled it up, and there she was. A girl in a fucking glass bottle."

"You're shitting us," Sarah said. "I don't believe you."

"It's true," Cat said. "I guess it was this girl that drowned like fifty years ago and her family wanted her buried in a bottle. She liked the water, or something."

"How old was she?" Sarah asked.

"Fifteen?" Cat said.

"Fifteen," Sarah said.

"What did she look like?" I asked. Cat glanced at Sarah, and she shrugged.

"You know," he said. He swirled the leftover ice in his glass. "Dead."

I imagined the girl in the bottle. The glass green and cool, lightly covered in quarry dust, pulled from the dirt. Inside perhaps dried flowers, crumbling when the first rush of cork-stopped air left the bottle and new breath entered: like a lung brought back to life. And the girl: lying as if asleep, with her dark hair pulled back from her forehead in slick waves. Or maybe she had copper tresses in a braid. Resting on her back, hands folded, a white gauzy dress falling just so over her shoulders. She would be an Ophelia, like we had learned in school. A river nymph, colored blue-green from the glass-filtered light.

"What did they do with her?" Sarah asked.

"Put it back in and covered it up," Cat said. "Since it's technically a grave. We can't touch it. It would be desecration."

Sarah drained her glass and set it on the floor. Cat's was already empty. I weighed my Coke can in my hand, thinking of what it would be like to be buried in one. Cold, and smelling of tin.

Sarah's phone buzzed. Cat looked at her, and she raised her eyebrows.

"A friend," she said. He nodded; she looked away. I thought there was a little extra color in her neck that I only saw when she was flustered, but the room was also overwarm from the sock-smelling radiator.

I had seen a dead person before: two years before, Gene's mother had died, and we'd gone to the wake, seen her bundled up in a red lacquered coffin. She did not look like a person—her skin was plastic and she looked much smaller than she should, like she'd been squeezed—so I had not been scared. I did not think the girl in the bottle would look like Gene's mother, though. I knew she would be dead, but she would also be not dead: asleep, maybe. I thought of how pale her skin would be, like the belly of a fish.

"Can we see her?" I asked. Cat and Sarah had their heads tucked together and did not answer so I asked my question again.

"No, man," Cat said, brushing his long hair out of his eyes. "I can't take you there. Rules, all that stuff." He smiled. Sarah's phone blinked; his smile undid just a little at the edge.

And then the afternoon went on in the way they always did: Sarah and Cat went to her room and shut the door, and I turned on the television with the volume louder than I needed it and occasionally rooted my hand around in my jeans furtively, twitching at any noise I heard. And when Gene and my mother came home with their arms full of hardware store bags and groceries, the door to Sarah's room was suddenly open and she and Cat were there blink-quick in the kitchen helping my mother unload the food and Gene was standing in the doorway asking me politely why I needed the television so loud. And on the screen was a woman in a red dress telling the camera that for the price of a chicken dinner our souls could be saved, if only we'd send the money in an envelope to an address in Missouri then the gates of Heaven would open to our knocking ghosts, and I imagined that standing next to those carved oak doors in the misty sky was the girl in the glass bottle, her hair dripping with dew and winking, waving, just for me.

.   .   .

A few days after Cat told us about the girl, I sat in the family room and picked at my puzzle with the television on mute. In the kitchen my mother was slicing something, and every so often I could hear an especially loud thwock on the cutting board. A contained sound, much like my mother.

Sarah entered in a bathrobe, her hair in a towel. She sat on the couch and took down her hair, then spread a magazine onto her lap. She had her phone in one hand, and she held it like she might a cigarette, with a lazy ease. It buzzed occasionally, lighting up her palm so that it glowed pink, reddish.

I kept my eyes on the television, set to a local news channel; on the screen a dozen thumb-sized mug shots rearranged themselves like shuffling cards. Eleven men and one woman, all smiling. I wondered if anyone had told them to smile, or if they'd decided among themselves. As the sound was muted—one of my mother's before-dinner rules—I could only imagine the story that might go along with them: a bank robbery; a murder mystery.

"Look," I said. "It's the meth heads." I nudged Sarah and pointed. She glanced up, then back down to the magazine she was riffling through.

"Not meth heads," she said.

Her continued refusal to recognize the problem we had was beginning to surprise me.

"This is a documented phenomenon," I said, trying

to keep the pity out of my voice. "You can't pretend it doesn't exist."

Sarah was quiet, flipping through the glossy pages.

"What do you think," she suddenly asked me, "should I look like this?" She tossed the magazine down to where I sat so I could see the spread: a girl smiling open-mouth wide, a boy draped over her shoulder. Her lips were shellacked pink and her teeth were as white as the text that read SHOW HIM YOUR MOVES. Her hands gripped the collar of her white button-down as if she were going to rip it open—the half-wink on her face suggested she knew the shirt would eventually succumb on its own to the force of the cleavage that strained against it. The boy was sullen and tan and carried, inexplicably, a fishing rod.

"Well?" Sarah persisted. She grimaced painfully, and I saw she was doing an imitation of the girl on the page. "Is this right?"

I wasn't sure why she was asking me; I could tell she was angry, but I couldn't tell about what. She seemed insistent that I give her a specific response.

"I like her teeth," I offered. "She has nice teeth."

Sarah frowned. I could see I had disappointed her. I thought of what I might do to redeem myself.

"I bet she swallows," I said.

I knew immediately it was wrong. Sarah looked at me as though I'd slapped her. On the television, the mug shots on the screen shuffled again. I realized there was no woman among the photos: it had only been a man with long hair.

"Why would you say that?" Sarah said, and now there was on her face a look I'd never seen: not anger, not sadness. Something much worse.

My neck was overwarm. "I don't know," I said. And I didn't. I only had remembered the look on the face of the boy who'd said it, a boy a few years older than me, who I had heard talking about my sister on the bus. I had not heard all of what they said but I did hear this one thing, and when he said it I caught the look on his face and was struck by the blend of reverence and something else—that hungry look Cat had sometimes when he looked at Sarah. Everything at war on his face.

"Where did you hear that?" Sarah asked.

I twisted, twisted. Oh, she had me on the hook. "Around," I told her. "Maybe some guys on the bus?"

She looked at me, a long measured look. "Who were they talking about?" she asked then, curious. I said nothing. And with every second I remained quiet her face became more still and withdrawn until it was as if she'd pulled a second face over hers and was someone quite different, though the bones were the same underneath.

I clicked the channel changer and the mugshots disappeared. A whaling schooner tilted across the screen.

"You think the girl in the bottle is very tall?" I asked. She ignored me.

That night after dinner I washed dishes with my mother. Gene sat at the table drawing a bench he planned to build. Sarah appeared at the door, ready to leave. She had lined her eyes with something dark and her lips were red and shiny.

"I'm going out," she said. My mother scrubbed at a dish fiercely.

"Watch out for the meth punks," I reminded Sarah. She rolled her eyes.

"Sarah," Gene said. She turned to face him, a hand on her hip, impatient, but she stood still for him. He paused.

"With Cat?"

"No," Sarah said. She shook her hair out from her shoulders and stared at Gene as though she were challenging him about something, but he only nodded.

"You know what's best," he said. My mother wrenched the dish from the water and passed it to me, slopping water on my arms. I flinched from the hot ceramic, but she did not seem to notice. I thunked the dish down to let my mother know she'd hurt me, but still she kept her hands in the sink, now making a lot of noise with the scattered utensils against the aluminum sides.

Sarah was quiet, for a moment, then said, "I do." And then she left the house, with only her fresh-shower smell and the skeeting sound of cicadas from the quick-opened door behind her.

.   .   .

And now, weeks later: the smashed car window. Sarah slim and quiet at the garage door while I purloined the shovels, whispering at me to put myself in gear.

The roads were empty, the sky an indigo scratched with the black outlines of tree branches reaching over the road like long spindly bones. The air rushed through the hole in Sarah's window and made it feel as though everything in the cabin were lifting up, about to take off. The shovels at my feet knocked with a scrapey sound every time we hit a bump.

"Cat's going to meet us there," Sarah said. "He's got a key."

I nodded calmly to let her know I'd heard, but secretly I was thrilled.

"Whatever," I said. I suspected Sarah knew more

about my excitement than I wanted her to, but she did not say anything, and we continued on in silence.

The quarry was at the end of a road that passed through the forest until the pines suddenly stopped, and you were coasting along a flat dusty plain where the trees had been cleared and a long chain-link fence cut the horizon off. The moon shone off the dusty ground and lit everything up, so it was white and gray and barren, like the surface of the moon, the light finding any angle to bounce off and make starker than it would be in the daytime. The night turned every surface into shadow and stone. It was beautiful, and horrible. I felt suddenly alone, even with Sarah beside me. As though we were castaways in some strange world. I wondered what she saw, what she felt—if it was the same as me, or something I couldn't even imagine.

"Do you think," I said to her, "that the girl in the bottle could float? If we put her on the water?"

"I think you're not really getting it," Sarah said. "She's dead."

"I am aware of that fact," I said.

"Are you really?" Sarah asked, sharp in a way I did not expect or quite understand, sharp like I'd offended her.

We reached the fence; Sarah pulled the car over and parked. She sat for a moment, the engine ticking as it cooled. At her knee she picked at a frayed patch on her jeans, twisting the threads and then jerking them up, puckering the fabric as it tugged. I watched the shovels gleam in the moonlight at my feet.

"Sam," Sarah said. "There weren't any meth heads. It was Cat that broke the window."

She had her head turned to me, and although I couldn't see her face clearly, I could imagine what it would look like: her brows slightly furrowed, the rest of her features serene. My sister had always been private about her emotions. It made me wonder, occasionally, if she even had them.

"Why do you keep blaming him?" I asked.

"Someday, you'll get it," she began, and I could not stand her then.

"Do you even like him at all?" I said, painfully aware that my voice was wavering with the fullness of my indignation: for Cat, for her insistence on his guilt. "I don't think you do!"

Sarah started to say something—her mouth a dark circle, paused; I could tell how badly she wanted to snap at me—but then there was a sweep of light and another engine rumbling into silence, and Cat was rapping at my window, saying "What's up, excavators? We gonna dig tonight?"

Cat led us into the dark. We followed him down a gravel path that cricked under our feet like ice; I trusted that he knew where he was taking us, as we could see only vague outlines around us in the dark, huge shapes that looked like fallen mastodon or enormous spindly insects. When the clouds crossed the moon we were plunged into pitch black and then, eyes blinking, would see some patch suddenly illuminated: twisty metal bits on the ground; a single thin wire strung across the path. The backbone of a giant object with sabered prongs tilted cattywompus in the dirt.

"Forklifts," Cat said, turning to us briefly, as though he'd known what I was looking at. "We let the machines sleep at night. So they don't turn against us." He laughed, a jangly sound I did not like; it might have been the darkness of the night or the eeriness of the quarry—the mounds of crushed stone, the alien landscape we crossed over—but I did not think Cat was, just now, the Cat I knew.

And then Cat stopped so abruptly I walked into his back, caught the musty, greeney smell of his coat, tobacco and a moist, fungal strain.

"Watch out," Sarah whispered beside me, something smug in her voice that it made me think that she'd been out here before with Cat, although he'd always told me he was not allowed to bring people to the quarry.

"Watch yourself," I said, as savagely as I could.

"Kids," Cat said, and we became quiet, and I then saw what he had brought us to see: the lip of the quarry. Cat stood in front of us, his arms outstretched, and at first it seemed as though the path continued on before him as it should, but then the shadows cleared away, and I saw that the ground dropped away in a straight, sheer line, and we were on the very edge of the crater. It seemed to go on for miles in front of us, a hollow scoop of the land that went down into blackness; deep divots pocked the walls where the daily drilling happened, where the workers were mining the quarry for better, deeper stone. Small trees clung to the edges of the gash, their roots visible where they threaded in and out of the dirt. It was not possible to see the bottom.

Sarah went to the edge and stood with Cat, an arm around his waist.

"Where does it end?" she asked.

"Where it begins," he said, his voice dreamy. I puzzled over that answer and decided I would not ask for clarification.

"It's trippy," Sarah said. "It's like an ocean, only with air."

"The fullness of emptiness," Cat said. "The movement of stillness."

"The bullshit of philosophy," Sarah said. I frowned at her sourness. I had been enjoying Cat's declarations, which seemed to me like they were close to something wise. Sarah was dampening everything, and I was near to letting her know about it but thought I would wait a little. I could be judicious when I tried.

"Oh," Cat said, fondly, "live a little." He kissed her forehead and walked back from the edge, leaving her standing there, silhouetted against the wide basin. I could only see a little silver sheen on her hair to tell that she was looking out at the quarry and not at us.

"Sarah," I said, "Come on." The silver wavered a little. Her back very straight, very still.

We continued. The path sloped and turned again and again and soon I could see we were following a hairpin route down into a level area of the quarry where the ground was packed flat and, though not the very bottom of the crater, was now shadowed by the high cliff walls. Cat followed the trail with a meandering grace that suggested either he was drunk or so familiar with the path he did not need to bother keeping straight: he would get to our destination by instinct or grace.

"Almost there," he kept saying, an incantation under his breath, the shovels at a jaunty angle on his shoulder, "almost there, almost there."

And then: we were there. The path ended in a low-slung sort of way, the ground flat and even with track marks from the big machines, like a gigantic bootmark in the dirt. A forklift waited in the shadows and there were butter-pat mounds of dirt scattered about. And like that, seeing those mounds of dirt, I recalled why we'd come, and my stomach swooped with excitement, sick and hot and thrilling.

Cat leaned against one of the forklift prongs; I heard a click-clicking and then there was his face lit by a Bic flame, then that white-black moon darkness again, and a glowing cigarette cherry. I heard him inhale, exhale. The most wonderful sound in the world. I had the fervent hope that someday I might be the type of person who could walk about in smoke and flame the way that Cat did.

Sarah sat on the ground and made little doodles with a stick. I thought she'd been very quiet for a while.

"Do you know, Cat," I said, "Sarah had a run-in with some punks tonight."

"Some punks, huh?" Cat said.

"Meth heads," I said. "They're everywhere. And they got her."

"Oh, shut up," Sarah said.

"What'd they do?" Cat asked. The cherry dipped, rose. Smoke in the air that wisped away with each word of his question.

"They smashed her car window," I said proudly. "Kapow! Smashed it up good."

"Kapow, is that right?" Cat said, but directed this at Sarah. She was silent, still scratching in the dirt with the stick. "I wonder why they would do that."

"Do you wonder that, Cat?" Sarah said, looking up from the ground. Her hair shimmered silver; the cherry glowed red.

"Oh," Cat said, his voice all casual, "I bet those meth punks got a little riled up about something. If you gave them a reason to be sorry, I bet they would."

"A reason to be sorry," Sarah said. "I bet they'd like

that."

"Smashed to smithereens," I said, trying to redirect the conversation back to its origins, impatient that somehow Cat seemed not to have gotten the full impact of the story.

"Well, then." The cherry went out; Cat stepped out of the darkness toward me. The shovels on his shoulder jostled, and I saw he carried his own sledgehammer with the skull-stone head. "Let's find this girl before those meth punks get back, hey?"

He grabbed the shovels and held one out to me. I took it, gripped the rough wood staff. It was warm from where his hands had been. When we uncovered the girl in the bottle, I thought, the noise from the shovels hitting the glass would be like the ringing of a bell.

"Cat," Sarah said. And in her voice I recognized something dangerous—there was nothing particular about it, but it was the firmness that made me perk my ears. She stood, put her hands in her pockets. "I don't want you to do this."

"Aw," Cat said, "it's just for fun. A little peek."

"Think about it," I said to Sarah. "A *girl* in a *bottle*."

Sarah shook her head. "No," she said. "No."

Cat leaned on his shovel. "You asked me to do it," he said. "We're here. We're here for this."

"Well, I don't want you to anymore," she said.

He laced his fingers together over the shovel's handle. "You don't *want* me to," he said. "What a request."

"I mean it," Sarah said. "This isn't right."

"You've got nerve, I'll give you that," Cat said.

I held my shovel at the ready, uncertain of what was happening between my sister and Cat, impatient with Sarah's sudden balking.

"What's your problem?" I asked her.

"It's not right," she said. She held a hand to me; I realized she wanted the shovel. "Sam. Come on."

I looked at Cat. He stood waiting, clicking the lighter on-off, on-off. The flame made glints on his jacket zipper. I thought of the girl in the bottle, how good it would feel to pull the green glass from the dirt, dust it off and look inside.

"Where is it?" I asked Cat.

We dug in a patch of moonlight where the dirt was already lumped up, soft and easy to fling away. I followed the methodical movements Cat made, not ever seeming to extend much energy or effort but removing huge chunks of soil, though my own work was scattered and small. But soon enough the ground was flat, and then there was a divot, and then a deep hole, so deep I had to bend far over to reach the soil.

"Should we prop it up when we get it out, or lay it flat?" I asked Cat.

"Oh, good question," Sarah said from behind me where she sat on the ground.

Cat ignored her. "I'm gonna jump on in here," he said to me, lowering himself down into the hole, "and push it up." With his shovel he made a few probing stabs at the ground until, suddenly, we heard it: a dull clanking sound.

Cat froze. "She's still there," he said, his voice reverent. We all waited. There was no wind in the trees, no sound at all. Nothing in the wide deep quarry except what we thought to ourselves.

Then Cat knelt, began to brush away the dirt with his hands. At first there was just a flurry of dust and then, slowly, I saw the outline of a bottle, maybe as long as I was tall, canted upward so the neck was slightly higher than the body.

"If you pull that bottle out," Sarah said. "If you do this. Cat, I swear."

"Get ready to hold it," Cat said, and like that he'd lunged his arms under the soft dirt and was pushing the bottle up, up and out of the hole toward me, a ship coming in to land, sliding over the packed quarry ground and settling into the thin gravel. The bottle was big, much bigger than I had ever expected, with a short, thick neck, and coated with dirt, dusty pale dirt that obscured what was in it. I thought I could smell something but wasn't sure. The bottle was big and there.

Cat climbed from the hole. "You ready?" he asked me. There were blotches of color high in his cheeks and he was breathing hard, an excited sort of hard. "You want to see?"

I approached the bottle; Cat knelt next to it, one hand resting on the curving top.

"She's in there," he said, looking at the bottle as though it were a deep lake, black water you could only just see through, and he the explorer about to dive. And then he began to dust the bottle off, brushing his hands over it carefully, lovingly, until I could see the dark green color of the glass appear first mutely, and then glowing, shiny beneath the moon that had not yet been covered by clouds. Under Cat's working hands the bottle took shape, a thing of his creation. I moved closer until I was just behind him looking over his shoulder. The green bottle seemed to pulse: Cat's shadow on it, a flickering wave.

Sarah spoke then. "Don't look, Sam," she said. "Remember what I told you? She's dead."

"Shut up, Sarah," I said. I decided she could just sit and simmer and stop distracting us with whatever mood she'd gotten into.

Cat took his hands from the bottle, sat back. "Ok," he said. And I stepped from behind him, so I could see the girl in the bottle.

At first I saw nothing, only the glass reflecting my face at me, and I frowned to see it, my nose distorted and my ears bulbous from the bottle's curve. But when my face faded away I could see the glass as itself, and then through the glass into the murk, a swampy type of substance pushing against its container, and floating in it all were large clumpy shapes of something pale. Cat touched the side of the bottle and it rocked slightly and, with my hand on the top, I could feel the weight of things gently moving inside, tremors sending out their forces through the muddy liquid. Still I concentrated, trying to find the girl, her long hair, a hand reaching for us, only there was just this thickness, impenetrable. Reeds and grass, yellowy fluid. Ophelia's grave emptied. I looked for the girl, for something looking back at me, but could not see it.

"Where is she?" I asked. I was very cold and wished my jacket were thicker. "Where's the girl?"

"Sam," Cat said, and put his arm around my shoulders, a touch I thought I would remember my entire life. And I looked harder into the bottle and then suddenly— horribly, suddenly—those clumpy shapes made sense to me. How could I ever say what I saw there? There was a girl in a bottle, and she was dead. I tried to stifle a noise coming from my lungs rising up into my throat, but I could not, and it came out anyway. I clamped my teeth down on it hard, trapped it in my mouth and choked. Cat put his hand on my chest and pushed me back a little, rose in a fluid motion and stared down at the bottle.

"How'd you think they got her in there, kid?" he asked me.

I stumbled away from the bottle, toward Sarah; I wished to put my head in her lap as I had used to do long ago and cry, let her comfort me. But her mercy was gone, the way she looked at me, and I remembered that my sister was not only my sister but a woman who was beautiful and cold.

"Are you satisfied?" she asked. She stood and walked to me, hard-faced Sarah. "Are you happy with yourselves now?"

"I didn't know," I said.

"Didn't know?" She laughed. "Don't even try to say that. I told you over and over."

"Leave him alone," Cat said.

"Oh?" Sarah moved across the flat ground and stood a pace away from Cat; in the moonlight they were dark bodies, symmetrical: their hair long and silver, tall and thin. Both poised against each other.

"You should not have done this," Sarah continued. "You should have known better. You could have said no, but you had to be you." As she said this, even as I still wanted to throw myself against her and make her forgive me, even as I knew we had done something terrible and felt myself incapable of forgiveness—I was alone, ugly to myself—I felt my heart swell for Cat, for the indignation of these accusations.

"Why won't you leave *him* alone?"

She turned, surprised. I could not stop now so I kept going. "He didn't break your car, and it's not his fault now. Why do you hate him?" I stumbled on. "Why do you—why do you *do* things with him if you don't like him?" I held the word back for as long as I could. "He loves you, and you're a slut."

The bottle sat there watching us. At the top of the cliff walls on the opposite side of the quarry, the moon fell behind a row of pines. The shadows jumped up. I blinked, unable to see.

"You stupid little kid," Sarah said. "It was Cat with the brick. It was always only Cat."

A click, a flash: the cigarette lit Cat's face from beneath. He took a single pull and flicked the stub away. It hit the bottle and the green sparked bright for a second. Cat spoke, and though he spoke to me he looked at Sarah.

"It was me, Sam," he said. "No meth heads. Just me."

My sister nodded at Cat. Their bodies leaned toward each other though they did not move. And I was ashamed. My sister, in love. I had never known.

"I won't change for you," Sarah said. "I won't."

"I know," he said.

We three stood there in the quarry. The bottle cool and green in the dirt. I did not want to look at it, but it sat there, the shovels keeled over by its side. The walls of the cliff were high, and I remembered that we would have to hike back up and out of this place, carrying everything we'd brought with us.

Cat brought his arm down. "Let's go home," he said; he went and gathered the shovels and hoisted them onto his shoulder and stood, waiting, looking at me.

"You coming?" he asked me.

Sarah had not moved. She was quiet, her arms wrapped tight around her. She shivered once, her form straight and tall, and said nothing to us. I had the sudden thought of Sarah standing there forever, the quarry around her filling with water while she waited — for what? I could not tell, though I thought I was close to seeing my sister, just then, as she was to herself. I wondered how many people had seen her like this. I wondered was this how Cat saw her, or my mother, or Gene, or anybody in the world, strangers who saw my sister passing through.

Cat held the shovels. I called to my sister, but she did not answer. Sarah was willful but she was not stupid, and I knew she would follow us eventually, make her own way up out of the quarry and join us where Cat and I would be sitting by the cars. She was sure to follow us. She would.

I looked behind to see if she was coming.

"Sarah?" I asked. I felt her outline turn to me in the darkness. Around us: the wrested dirt, the bottle. The gaping hole in the ground. A wind started, a steady wind that swept along the quarry walls chasing noise before it, and the cavernous space was full of that sound as it blew. A low whistle, a voice. It died and began again, and we stood there listening to it. That quarry wind, the loneliest sound in the world. The way it blew—so pure, persistent, carving away bit by bit at the walls and the floor and the rocks and dirt. Taking all the time it needed to do its work removing every grain of every stone, until eventually there would be none left at all.

HOW NOT TO MESS UP THE SEATING PLAN AT YOUR WEDDING

Anita Goveas

HOW NOT TO MESS UP THE SEATING PLAN AT YOUR WEDDING

Anita Goveas

Manjira slammed the lid of the boot, Taj yanked his fingers away.

'Hey, your friend came on to *me*. You forgot the tapioca.'

She stabbed the boot-latch, broke her nail.

"Olena can't speak to guys. She turns red and stammers."

A stench pervaded the car. The dessert sloshed, sweetened muck in a box. The smell was stronger than that.

"Maybe she was drunk."

Something feral and musky made her lungs twitch. She needed to find the source.

"She doesn't drink, Taj."

A drop of brown fluid had invaded, it was spreading. It stank of rotting meat.

"There you go, someone spiked her lassi, made her horny."

The drop continued its destructive path. She should mop it up, before it did real damage.

"She's not a bridesmaid, just seat her far away at the wedding. Problem solved, Manji."

Her seventeen-year-old, peach-breasted sister was a bridesmaid. She threw the box in, slammed the lid again. No time to clean up, people were waiting.

PORCHES

Alison Closter

PORCHES

Alison Closter

First, complain politely. Tell them that their florescent paint job isn't your cup of tea. Alabaster, ivory or pearl would be a much more appropriate color for this neighborhood. But yellow is the color of the future, the wife shouts from her adjacent porch. Don't you want to be surrounded by sunshine?

When the husband gets out his chainsaw and a ladder and starts sawing branches off the old oak tree, the very tree your father planted the year before his death, call the police. The husband plays innocent. I thought it was our property, he says. Besides, the tree is dead anyway.

Offer the police coffee and blueberry pie. Tell them your father was on the force, even though he took an early retirement. Tell them your great grandfather founded this town, and he would never stand for *these* sort of people moving in. The police look bored. They have never heard of your father or grandfather. Ask them to protect the tree. Realize as they smile and nod and leave their pie unfinished that they will do nothing.

When some tomatoes go missing from the back garden—picked clean from the vine while you were busy fixing tuna sandwiches for your nephew—consider calling the police again.

Watch the neighbors' shadows duck and cower behind the curtains as their voices assault your home at an unacceptable volume. Listen for your name. You introduced yourself once when they first arrived. They have probably forgotten who you are. But of course they must talk about you.

The son uses a donkey piñata for target practice in their front lawn, shredding the creature into bite sized bits. You hope a bullet ricochets and takes his eye out. Feel the blood rise to your cheeks. You have never had violent thoughts before. You're a good citizen. It's them. They're the problem. If only the husband would fall asleep with his lit cigarette.

When the son wakes you with his rap music, revving the engine of his Chevy in the street, go to their door. As sweet as you can, inform them that this isn't a dance club and you have to be at the library early. The husband says, It's nine o'clock. Who goes to bed at nine o'clock? The wife blows cigarette smoke in your face. Boys with their toys, the wife giggles in this childish way, a sad sound that reminds you of your friend, Flora, who jumped from a moving vehicle, your vehicle, on the New Jersey turnpike. No grown woman should laugh like that, you told Flora before the accident. Oh, she said. Teach me how to laugh the right way. You cannot remember the last time you laughed.

Later, you hear the wife scold the teenage son. At last, you think, the woman is taking some responsibility. But then she tells him, Wear your seatbelt! You've been drinking! Give up on decency.

Why they have let their garbage accumulate in the yard: tires, empty beer cans, a ripped mattress, a broken baby carriage—befuddles you. They say they won't cut the grass because they're afraid of poison ivy, but it grows so tall that your cats get lost in it. Skunks and raccoons roam free. Once the rats start to congregate, call animal control. From your front stoop, watch uniformed men arrive and give the husband a warning. Across the way, he stares at you. You're worse than a bag full of rattlesnakes, he coughs, then spits. Curse him, silently.

Go to the pet store and buy a plastic bag full of crickets. Cut a small hole in their screen door and send the crickets in to wander the crevices of their home. It's early morning, two hours before the sun comes up, and those crickets will sing to eternity.

Leave a typed note in their mailbox: *Have you discovered what lives in the walls? You will.*

When the police come to accuse you of horrible things, smile and refill their coffee cups. Then, slip them the "get out of jail free" card from the Monopoly game you used to play with your brother. Those were the days when he hurled the board off the table, and the pieces scattered, just as you began to win.

FATHER
VS SON

Chistopher James

FATHER VS SON

Chistopher James

Father and son have a race, and both run faster and harder than they've ever run before. But they forgot to decide upon a finishing line, so neither wants to stop, and they keep going, running forever or until one of them dies.

You're going to die first, says the son. You're old, and overweight, and you have heart problems. And man flu.

You'll die first, says the father. You drink too much, and you smoke, and you're overweight too.

But I'm less overweight than you. And I stopped smoking.

Well woopty fucking doo.

This went on. We can call this concern. Sometimes the concern didn't hurt. When the son told the father he was old, the father could take this. No shit, Columbo. He *was* old, his *friends* were old, his *wife* was old, *everyone* was old in his world. But it hurt when the son told the father his violent temper had made growing up a nightmare. When he said he'd pretended to be an orphan his first day at school. When the father told the son he'd end up like his cousin Frank if he didn't stop drinking. I've already stopped drinking, thought the son, which was more or less true. More less true, perhaps.

They tried to keep the concern from being too barbed, because the shame and hurt and anger made the other person run faster. It was easier on their legs to say you'll die because you've not seen the inside of a gym since Michael Jordan made Space Jam.

This wasn't the only race they'd run. Example: the son was eighteen, the father driving them back from somewhere. Someone was a little slow on a roundabout and the father honked the horn, shouted something. The son was embarrassed and didn't talk to the father again the rest of the ride. The father realized and didn't talk to the son. They got home and still didn't talk. The father went out into the garden to check on his strawberries, and the son made him a cup of tea. Didn't tell the father, left the tea in the kitchen. The tea went cold, and the son knew the father wouldn't drink it. He turned on the TV, found a show his father would like, then went to another room to read the papers. The father came back, made a fresh cup, switched the TV off, read the papers in his own room. Still didn't talk. Finally the son forgot they weren't talking, and he shouted out something to his father about what that idiot prime minister had done now. The tea you made me, the father shouted back, you let it go cold. The father won that one, but he wouldn't win this.

Example: everyone, I mean everyone, asked the son to apologize to his father for something. The son couldn't remember what, but he'd never said he was sorry. The son had won that.

You should stop here, said the son. We're getting pretty far.

I don't mind still going, said the father. But you can stop if you're worried about getting back.

No, I'm okay.

Yeah, I'm okay too.

There was a mother somewhere behind them, way behind them by now. The father assumed the mother was supporting him except for the times he assumed she'd be rooting for their son. The son, of course, knew the mother would be on his side. Wasn't she the one who'd always come to his room to tell him not to cry? You know what your father's like, she'd say.

They had also raced over gardening. The father had won, by a Roman mile. They'd raced over music. The son had smashed that one. They'd raced over cooking, ending in a tie, except for Japanese cooking, which the son had edged. The son had won taste in movies, the father in being handy. The son had done and enjoyed many drugs, and the father had smoked pot once and thrown up, so it was unclear who'd won there. The son had won not being racist, though the father had held his ground a lot longer than expected. The father had won having a proper job, working to support a family, and paying for the son's education, which he'd made little good use of. The son won moving abroad; the father hadn't even turned up for that.

There is no end to this race. The father did die, finally, but the race goes on.

[contributor bios]

A native of Wisconsin, **Bridget Apfeld** holds an MFA from the University of North Carolina at Wilmington, and a BA from the University of Notre Dame. She lives in Austin, TX and work as a production assistant at the University of Texas at Austin. Her previous and forthcoming work is featured in various journals, including *So to Speak*, *The Fem*, *Dislocate*, *Midwestern Gothic*, *Dappled Things*, *Newfound*, *Brevity*, and *Verse Wisconsin*. She is currently editing her second novel.

Suzanne Burns writes both fiction and poetry in Bend, Oregon and Paris, France. *The Chicago Tribune* recently published her short fiction.

Alison Closter teaches high school students literature and writing near Boston. She has previously published a short story in *Flying South Magazine*, and she has a flash fiction piece forthcoming in *Monkey Bicycle*.

Anita Goveas is British-Asian, based in London, and fueled by strong coffee and paneer jalfrezi. She lurks in libraries and her local independent bookshop, Bookseller Crow. She was first published in the 2016 *London Short Story Prize* anthology, most recently in *Pocket Change*, *Haverthorn*, *Moonchild Magazine*, *Riggwelter Press*, *Anti-Heroin Chic*, *former cactus mag*, and *Litro*. She tweets erratically @coffeeandpaneer

[contributor bios]

Chelsea Harris has appeared in *Literary Orphans*, *Smokelong Quarterly*, *Minola Review*, *The Fem*, *The Portland Review*, and *Grimoire*, among others. She received her MFA from Columbia College Chicago.

Christopher James lives, works and writes in Jakarta, Indonesia. He has previously been published online in many venues, including *Tin House*, *Fanzine*, *McSweeney's*, *SmokeLong*, and *Wigleaf*. He is the editor of *Jellyfish Review*.

Matt Kolbet teaches and writes in Oregon.

Sonal Sher was born in Srinagar, Jammu & Kashmir and did her education in Delhi, pursuing a bachelors in Physics from Hindu College. She worked for a not-for-profit organization Hippocampus Reading Foundation and as a journalist for *Deccan Herald* and *Hindustan Times*. Recently she wrote her first feature film, *Chidiakhana* produced by Children's Film Society of India. She is an alum of the UEA Creative Writing Course organized by University of East Anglia and was part of the first edition of New Writers' Mentorship Programme in Jaipur Literature festival 2017.

[contributor bios]

Emily Wortman-Wunder lives in Denver, Colorado. Her work has appeared in *Vela*, *Nimrod*, *Terrain*, *High Country News*, and many other places.

CPSIA information can be obtained
at www.ICGtesting.com
Printed in the USA
FFHW022330060119
50064015-54887FF